IBEN SANDEMOSE

GRACIE & GRANDMA

& THE ITSY, BITSY SEED

Translation by
Tonje Vetleseter

MACKENZIE
SMILES
San Francisco

THIS iS A STORY ABOUT AN iTSY, BiTSY SEED.

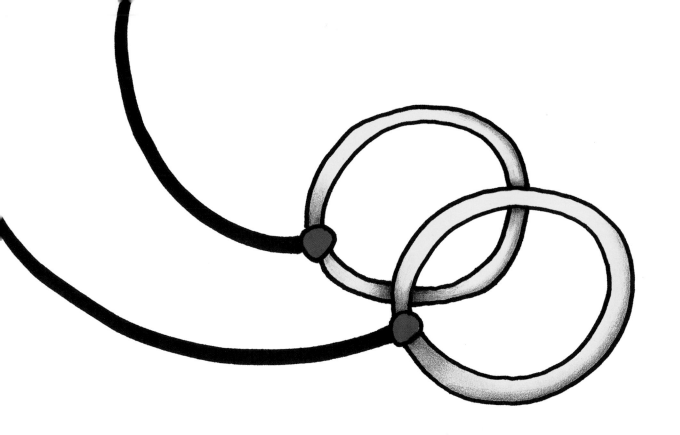

BUT IT IS ALSO A STORY ABOUT GRACIE,
WHO LOVES TO SWING SO FAST ON THE
RINGS THAT SHE LOOKS LIKE A FLYING
FISH SOARING THROUGH THE AIR.

AND IT'S ABOUT GRANDMA,
WHO JUMPS SO HIGH ON
GRACIE'S TRAMPOLINE THAT
PLANES AND SMALL BIRDS
SCREECH TO A HALT WHEN
SHE APPEARS IN THE SKY.

ONE DAY, WHILE IT WAS
STILL SPRING, GRACIE
BROUGHT GRANDMA A GIFT.
"MYSTERIOUS. WHAT IS IT?"
ASKED GRANDMA.
"JUST WAIT. YOU'LL SEE,"
SAID GRACIE. "BUT YOU HAVE
TO GIVE IT LOTS OF WATER!"

EACH DAY WHEN GRACIE ATE DINNER
AT GRANDMA'S HOUSE, SHE COULD SEE
THE GIFT HAD ENOUGH WATER TO DRINK.
"GRANDMA WILL NEVER GUESS WHAT IT IS.
I AM THE ONLY ONE WHO KNOWS,"
SMILED GRACIE.

"THIS GIFT IS THIRSTY," SAID GRANDMA. "IT JUST WANTS MORE WATER. SOON IT WILL GROW THROUGH THE ROOF! HAVE YOU GIVEN ME A BANANA TREE? OR A TREE WITH LEMONS? A BUSH WITH FRIED MACKEREL, MAYBE?"

BUT GRACIE SAID NOTHING. ONLY *SHE* KNEW THE SECRET.

GRANDMA MOVED THE GIFT OUT TO THE
BALCONY. SHE DIDN'T HAVE TO WATER
IT SINCE ALL THROUGH THE SUMMER
THE SUN WOULD SHINE ONE DAY AND
THE RAIN WOULD POUR DOWN THE NEXT.
THE PLANT GREW RIGHT INTO THE CLOUDS,
BUT NO BANANAS APPEARED.
"IT COULD BE A BALLOON TREE,"
GRACIE SUGGESTED, "WITH BALLOONS
THAT FLY US TO THE MOON!"
"DOES THAT EXIST?" GRANDMA WONDERED.

"NO, ACTUALLY THE BALLOON SEEDS WERE ALL SOLD OUT," SAID GRACIE. "THERE WAS JUST ONE SPIKY SEED LEFT, AND THAT WAS THE SEED OF A GIANT, SNARLING, DANGEROUS...

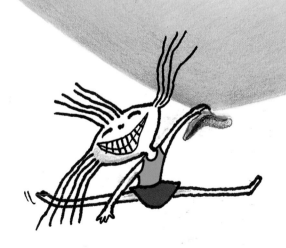

"...MONSTER TREE THAT EATS EVERYTHING!"

"OH, NO!" SAID GRANDMA, SHAKING.

"BUT I WILL SAVE YOU, OF COURSE," SAID GRACIE.

"BY THE WAY," GRACIE ADMITTED, "THERE WERE NO MORE MONSTER TREE SEEDS LEFT EITHER, JUST...

"...JUNGLE SEEDS!" GUESSED GRANDMA.
"I AM GETTING A JUNGLE ON THE BALCONY
WITH WILD CHOCOLATE PIGS AND GUMMY SNAKES."
"WRONG!" SAID GRACIE. "YOU WILL NEVER GUESS IT!"
GRANDMA WAS A LITTLE RELIEVED, SINCE BOTH
GORILLAS AND LIONS COULD GROW OUT OF
A JUNGLE SEED. "HOW ABOUT A . . .

"...COW TREE, THEN? THAT IS SURELY WHAT IT IS,"
GRANDMA SAID. "THEN I WILL ALWAYS HAVE
MILK FOR MY COFFEE. THANK YOU, GRACIE!"
BUT GRACIE JUST LAUGHED, "A COW TREE?
HOW SILLY. IT'S A...

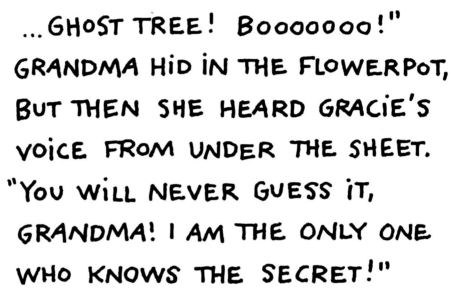

...GHOST TREE! BOOOOOOO!"
GRANDMA HID IN THE FLOWERPOT,
BUT THEN SHE HEARD GRACIE'S
VOICE FROM UNDER THE SHEET.
"YOU WILL NEVER GUESS IT,
GRANDMA! I AM THE ONLY ONE
WHO KNOWS THE SECRET!"

BUT ONE MORNING GRANDMA SPOTTED
SOMETHING NEW – A DOT. HIGH, HIGH
UP, NOT QUITE GREEN, NOT YELLOW,
EITHER. IT WAS, MAYBE, MOSTLY RED.
AND WHEN GRANDMA CLIMBED ALL
THE WAY UP TO THE TOP, SHE
SAW THAT IT WAS A...

...TOMATO!

"GRACIE!" GRANDMA CALLED DOWN FROM UP HIGH. "A BIG TOMATO!"

"WHAT ELSE?" GRACIE SHOUTED BACK.

"SHOULD WE MAKE KETCHUP OUT OF IT?" ASKED GRANDMA.

"NO," GRACIE ANSWERED. "WE WILL MAKE...

Mackenzie Smiles, LLC
San Francisco, CA

www.mackenziesmiles.com

Originally published as
Fiat og Farmor Hemmeligheten
by
© J.W. Cappelens Forlag A.S. 2004
www.cappelendamm.no

Original artwork & design by Iben Sandemose
The artwork in this book was drawn with ink and marker.

Translation by Tonje Vetleseter

Art production by Bernard Prinz

ISBN 978-0-9790347-5-6 41410621 9/09

Printed in China

10 9 8 7 6 5 4 3 2 1

Distributed in the U.S. and Canada by:
Ingram Publisher Services
One Ingram Blvd.
P.O. Box 3006
La Vergne, TN 37086
(888) 800-5918